THE INNKEEPER'S TALES

Humorous Stories about THE GLEN ROCK INN

Enjoy –
Nancy Welch

Nancy Turner Welch

ISBN 0-939241-94-3

ABOUT THE COVER

Special thanks to Brinkley Melvin, our "across the street" neighbor on Kentucky Road, in Montreat, North Carolina, for the beautiful cover photo of THE GLEN ROCK INN, in full bloom.

ABOUT THE AUTHOR

Nancy Turner Welch is the daughter of a Presbyterian minister from Ocala, Florida. She spent her summers in Montreat where her family owned a home.

Nancy is a graduate of Florida State University and holds a master's degree from Clemson University. She lives in Greer, South Carolina, where she is an active community leader.

Since 1966, she has hosted a TV show, THE NANCY WELCH SHOW, in upper South Carolina and is employed in higher education. She is the author of craft and cookbooks, collects antique quilts and is a popular, humorous speaker.

CONTENTS

INTRODUCTION

THE GLEN ROCK INN is located in Montreat, North Carolina. The Inn has a rich and interesting heritage dating back to the early 1800's. At that time, several men were looking for a retreat to get away from the "hustle and bustle" of Rutherford County, North Carolina life. They stumbled onto a beautiful stream, in the bottom of a "bowl" of mountains, near Asheville, North Carolina. As they developed their dream for a mountain retreat and continued to share their dream with others, the time came to make property available for private homes to be built. The stream was dammed up and a lovely Lake Susan was the result. Because everyone wanted lake front property and availability was limited, the decision was made that no one would have a lake front lot. This decision proved to be wise since this made the lake available for everyone to enjoy.

The story goes that near the end of the century, property away from the lake was divided into lots and numbered. At the appointed time, all of the numbers were put into a top hat and were drawn. If the person that drew a number wanted the lot, they paid a nominal amount and the property was theirs. If they didn't want the lot they drew, the number went back in the hat and their turn came after all others. The original owner of 421 Kentucky Road sold the property shortly after the drawing. The new owner, who was from Rutherfordton, built the original home in 1907. The house consisted of a living room, small dining room and kitchen on the first floor, along with a front porch. On the second floor, there were three bedrooms and one bathroom.

In the 1920's, Mrs. W.W. McCutchen purchased the cottage. She and her husband were from Bishopville, South Carolina, and the home gave her an opportunity to get away from the low country heat in the summer while her husband farmed. During the years of the Depression, Mrs. McCutchen opened her home to weary travelers looking for a place to stay for the night. For one dollar, a guest could have three meals and overnight accommodations. After the Depression, Mrs. McCutchen enlarged the house. Two bedrooms with a connecting bath, a large dining room and another kitchen were added on the first floor, and the front porch was extended the length of the house. The second floor gained seven bedrooms and two bathrooms. Mrs. McCutchen then named the house The Glen Rock Inn.

In 1948, C.T. and Tallulah Welch bought the Inn. They were friends of Mrs. McCutchen in Bishopville and they fell in love with the Inn and Montreat on their first visit. C.T. and Tallulah made some additions to the Inn during the years between 1948 and 1984. Five more baths were added upstairs and an additional dining room and another kitchen area were added downstairs. They also added two bedrooms and a bathroom under the front porch, affectionately called the dungeon!

In 1985, Charlie, the Welches' only child and I, their daughter-in-law, took over the Inn when C. T. and Tallulah were no longer able to manage it. We continued renovations by adding an apartment in the back of the Inn. This addition provided housing for the summer staff. Soon after, a white gazebo was added on the mountain creek, which has become a favorite resting spot.

There are now 14 bedrooms and 8 bathrooms in the Inn, and the dining rooms will seat 100 people. The 60-foot long front porch is usually full of people in white rocking chairs or in the big swing. I give you these details so you will understand that The Glen Rock Inn is really an old fashioned boarding house!

There is one other item that I must disclose. As I have already mentioned, C.T. and Tallulah lived in Bishopville, South Carolina. However, I haven't mentioned that a ghost, Dr. Baskins, inhabited their home on Church Street in Bishopville! Dr. Baskins built the large house and we believe he died in or near it well before the Welches' purchase in 1957. Even though they agreed he was a friendly ghost, each time something strange happened in the house, the Welches would say, "Dr. Baskins!"

During the summers, when the Welches were running the Inn, C.T. would make several trips from Montreat to Bishopville to harvest vegetables from his garden for the Inn.

On one of these trips, C.T. had finished in the garden and was going to fix supper. He entered the den and turned on the lamp and an oscillating fan that was on the floor. He went to the kitchen to start his supper. While his food was cooking, he returned to the den to watch TV. The room was dark and the fan was still. He remembered turning on the lamp and the fan and assumed he had blown a fuse. Before going to the breaker box to check, he reached for the lamp and turned the knob. To his surprise, the light came on. He reached down to turn on the fan again but the fan did not start. He looked at the fan, the switch and the cord. The cord had been unplugged from the wall!

"Okay, Dr. Baskins," C.T. spoke into thin air!

"I'm going to spend the night here, so leave me alone!" Dr. Baskins left him alone, that night!

There are many other stories about Dr. Baskins, but only one more to share at this writing.

When C.T. and Tallulah passed away, the home in Bishopville was sold to the City of Bishopville for offices. Some of the furniture from their home was moved to The Glen Rock Inn. Since Dr. Baskins had no place to live, he moved with the furniture! Well, at least some of us believe that. Others believe he stayed in the house in

Bishopville because during the remodeling, the builders were unable to keep the new plaster on the walls and after several attempts, they gave up and completely sheet rocked the house. The builder also said that during the remodeling, they had 27 hammers disappear!

Regardless of the claim that Dr. Baskins is still in Bishopville, a strange thing happened during the writing of this book. I was at The Glen Rock Inn during the fall of the year to host a group of people. While they were meeting, I decided I would begin work on this book. I pulled out my lap top computer, popped in a floppy disk and began writing the stories. About three hours later, everyone was ready to leave so I packed up as well.

I saved the text to the floppy disk and I saved the text to the hard drive. Several evenings later, back in South Carolina, I was going to continue the project. To my surprise, I had nothing on my floppy disk and nothing on my hard drive!

I shared my distress with the rest of my family.

"Dr. Baskins!" they voted, unanimously! "Don't work on the book at the Inn," they said, "or you'll never be able to finish it. He doesn't want you writing stories about the Inn!"

Not to be outdone by Dr. Baskins, the stories follow. They are stories from C.T. and Tallulah Welch or Charlie and me. They are shared in this book to be sure they will not be lost and will be enjoyed by those who love a good story, have known the Welches, or have loved THE GLEN ROCK INN.

1

THE FIRST GUEST

When Charlie and I began running the Inn in 1985, much cleaning and polishing was done to get ready to open for the summer. My good friend, Alice, had been helping in this process and was going to serve as the hostess that summer. On Sunday afternoon, Alice and I had finished everything. We stopped to rest on the porch and wait for our first guest to arrive. Alice turned to me and said,

"This is a Hallmark moment."

I said, "What do you mean?"

"Well, we are sitting here waiting for your first

guest to arrive. This is a special moment," Alice explained. I agreed and took a long breath, trying to savor the moment! Just at that time, a car pulled up in front of the Inn. Alice and I jumped to our feet and rushed down the stone path to the street to assist the older lady we were expecting. Much like a scene from *The Bob Newhart Show,* Alice and I were anxious to help. As our rather large guest opened the car door and started climbing out of the back seat, she didn't say hello or how do you do or even what her name was. Her first words were, "I've been constipated since I left Miami!"

The next morning, the lady asked me if there was a drug store in Montreat. I told her there wasn't one in Montreat anymore, but there was one in Black Mountain. She asked if someone could pick up some things for her the next time they went to town. I told her I would be glad to get whatever she needed. She said, "I need two Fleet enemas, and..." I interrupted her. "Why don't you just go with me to town and I can drop you off at the drug store when I go to the grocery store?" She said that would be fine. So after breakfast, Alice and I took the lady to town and she made her purchases.

After lunch, the lady told us that she was going to "take the afternoon off and get herself **straight!**"

When 6:00 pm arrived, we rang the dinner bell as usual. Alice came in the kitchen and said, "The lady we took to the store this morning hasn't come down for dinner. Should I go knock on her door?" I said that would be a good idea. Alice knocked on her door and told her that dinner was being served. When she came down she said, "I'm glad you came and got me. I had two Fleet enemas, two Valium and an aspirin and I didn't hear the bell!"

We were surprised she didn't hear St. Peter ringing the bell at the pearly gate!

2

MRS. STARK

One of the patrons of The Glen Rock Inn in the late 40's and early 50's was Mrs. Stark. She was from Mississippi and each year, she would make the trip to The Glen Rock Inn and spend at least part of the summer.

She told this as the truth! In Mississippi, she had seen a tombstone that read:

Ma loved Pa,

Pa loved the women,

Ma caught Pa with two in swimming.

Here lies Pa.

3

THE PIG

In 1989, we built an apartment at the rear of the Inn so that our summer staff would have a place to stay. We decided to make the apartment available for college students to rent during the winter because campus housing was at a premium. The first winter, we rented the apartment to the Montreat College basketball coach and his family. He left the college in the middle of the year and asked permission to sublet to his student assistant and her roommate. We agreed. For the next few years, we had a series of female students each year living in the furnished apartment. They were all great tenants.

In the fall of 1994, three new girls approached me about renting the apartment. They said they were students at Montreat College.

These attractive and vivacious girls were accepted as the others had been...without any recommendations from the college and with the total belief that they were, in fact, Montreat College students. Since we had never had any trouble from our previous renters, the thought never occurred to me to be suspicious.

One April evening, I went to the Inn to prepare for a luncheon the next day. As I was setting up the dining room, I noticed that the apartment was completely dark. There were no lights on and no cars were in the driveway. I told Charlie that I thought something was strange and that the girls might have moved out.

The next day, using our key, we opened the door of the apartment. A terrible smell and a notice informing us that the power had been disconnected due to a three-month delinquent bill greeted us! As Charlie and I walked into the apartment, we looked at the master bedroom and discovered the room had been completely trashed. There were broken beer bottles, broken mirrors, piles of nasty clothes, our broken chest of drawers and all kinds of debris everywhere. The queen-sized bed had obviously been the home for several cats! The floor of the master bathroom was a litter box that had not been cleaned out in months! The shower curtain was covered in black mold. The vanity counter had drug paraphernalia everywhere. The living room loveseats were peppered with cigarette burns. As if the visual sights weren't bad enough, the smell was just too overwhelming to describe.

The front bedrooms were in pretty good shape, but as I opened the door to the fourth bedroom, out ran a black, potbellied pig! I think I must have looked like his next meal! I ran out of the apartment and into the Inn and didn't stop until I got to the front porch! I was screaming all the way, "It's a PIG, it's a PIG, it's a PIG." Charlie came after me and when he realized what I was saying, he went back in the apartment to see if I was losing my mind. He entered the apartment only to hear and see the 75-pound pig in the living room! This was when we discovered the origin of the terrible smell!

The final outcome of this episode was that we never found the three girls and never got any financial help from them since we discovered they were in fact, not Montreat College students after all! Every fabric surface in the apartment had to be thrown away including the mattresses, curtains, upholstery on furniture and carpet. In fact, the floor had to be removed in the room where the pig had lived! The apartment was also infested with ticks! The cost of the repairs exceeded $5,000. As if all of this wasn't enough, the discovery was made just four weeks before our younger son, Nelson's wedding and eight weeks before the opening of the Inn for the summer.

Some people who have heard this story say, "The poor pig!" I say, "I don't think so!" The girls did move off and leave the pig behind however, they left him with a 25-pound bag of feed and a large bowl of water and they had only been gone three days. We took pictures and called the city manager. He carried the pig away in a bear cage to Old McDonald's farm in Black Mountain where, we assume, he lives happily ever after.

4

DISCRETION

For many years, there was a guest book that was faithfully kept at The Glen Rock Inn. In one of these books there is an entry without a name!

> I take my drinks with Discretion,
> One drink at Most.
> Two I'm under the table
> And Three, I'm under the Host!

5

THE SKATING RINK

Charlie and I had many house parties with friends from South Carolina. On one such occasion, the group had been enjoying adult beverages after a full day of shopping, golf, mountain climbing and bike riding. One of the men pointed out that he heard music coming from down the street and was going to find out what was going on. When Ronnie returned, he said there were people skating downstairs under the gym and it was free! He said,

"We can cream our butts for nothing!"

Several people ventured down the street to

try their "feet" at skating. One of the girls was wearing moccasins. She kept trying to attach the screw-on-skates to the moccasins and couldn't figure out why they hurt and wouldn't stay on!

Ronnie was the first to get the skates on and make the round on the concrete floor. Not even half way around the rink, he fell. He was wearing a white velour shirt, which was soon partially covered in blood from the huge gash in his forehead. He was quickly brought back to the Inn and we began trying to determine who was sober enough to drive him to the hospital in Asheville. Charlie was selected to drive, but two doctors, who were also guests, insisted on riding to the hospital with them. Neither doctor was sober!

The injured man, Ronnie, kept saying his arm hurt. Knowing that he was not one of the sober guests, the group kept reassuring him, "Your head is hurt, not your arm. See the blood on your shirt? That is from your head, not your arm." Every few minutes, he would repeat, "My arm hurts," and each time, we would jointly say,

"It's your head, not your arm, that is hurt." While in the emergency room, others that were more seriously injured kept getting in front of Ronnie. Finally, one of our not-so-sober doctors said, "Give me a needle and I'll stitch him up. I'm a doctor!"

The emergency room nurse said,

"What kind of doctor are you?"

"We are both gynecologists," he replied, pointing to the other not-so-sober doctor. With that, she said, "Sorry, guys. That's the wrong end!"

Eventually Ronnie was successfully stitched up and returned to the Inn. He continued to say his arm was hurting, and everyone continued to blow him off!

The following week, we received a call from Ronnie saying he had gone to the doctor in Greenville, and he indeed had a broken arm!

6

C.T.'S THYROID

Sometime in the 50's, C.T. Welch had part of his thyroid removed. Instead of having the surgeon dispose of this interesting collectable body part, C.T. had the thyroid put in a jar of formaldehyde! What an interesting conversation piece! Our children, Turner and Nelson, always wanted to see the jar when they would go to the Inn as C.T. carried the jar to the mountains in the summer and to Bishopville in the winter. This was, apparently, his badge of courage or his security "blanket"!

7

THINGS THAT GO BUMP IN THE NIGHT

Since I was an interior design major at Florida State University, having 18 bedrooms to redecorate was one of the most enjoyable aspects of owning The Glen Rock Inn. Each year, during the winter, I tried to redo at least two bedrooms completely including wallpaper, curtains and bed linens.

I had everything together to redecorate two bedrooms when I arrived late one afternoon. I was prepared to work until I finished. I had stopped in town to get some supper. By the time I got to the Inn, dark had caught me and I unloaded the car with only the spotlight in the yard.

The room that was to be transformed that night was on the upstairs hall. I had been working for several hours. The wallpapering had been completed, and I was on the floor, trimming above the baseboard, when I heard a strange knocking. Since I was "home alone" this noise was a bit disturbing. I looked out the window at the back of the house and saw nothing in the parking lot below and nothing at the back door. Trying to convince myself that I just <u>thought</u> I had heard something, I got back on the floor and back to my business of trimming the wallpaper. A few minutes later, I heard the same strange knocking sound. This time the noise <u>did</u> sound as if something was knocking on a door or wall but I couldn't determine the exact direction from where the sound was coming. I went to the <u>front</u> of the house and looked out. Because of the overhang of the front porch, I could not see if there was someone at the front door. I waited to see if anyone would walk down from the front porch and onto the street where I would be able to see them. Again, nothing!

I returned to my trimming job around the baseboards. By this time, I was practically lying down on the floor in the doorway of the bedroom. Suddenly, out of the corner of my eye, I saw something move in the bathroom across the hall. Then I heard the strange sound again. This time, I was up close and personal with the sound!

I had made a trip to the Inn to check the measurements for wallpaper and curtains a few days earlier. The house had been closed up for several months and on the counter by the telephone I had seen evidence of mice! When I returned this time, I had brought plastic 4" square trays with 2" squares of poison in them to place where I had seen the droppings. I had put out several of these trays throughout the house, including in the bathroom across the hall.

I saw the plastic tray with the square of poison moving across the floor and banging into the wall. The sound was coming from a rat (not a mouse) that was pushing the tray and was hitting the bathroom wall. I never saw the rat, only the edge of the tray moving. Any rat that was big enough to move that tray could have the Inn for the night! I turned off the lights, got my things and drove home!

8

GNATS

When Tallulah, the owner of the Inn, was in high school, she worked during the Christmas holidays in a department store. One day a large black woman came into the store. When Tallulah asked if she could help her, she said she wanted to see the bloomers.

"Do you want the kind with or without elastic in the legs?" Tallulah asked.

"<u>With</u> elastic," she said emphatically. "The gnats is so bad."

9

SILK

I was with friends of mine, Leigh and Ginna, and we had just completed a full day of shopping. I had one more stop to make before calling it quits. Earlier in the month, I had been in this interior design shop to look for drapery material. As we opened the door about 10 minutes before 5:00 pm, the owner of the shop (later to be called Silk) looked up from her desk, where she was obviously checking up for the day, and said,

"Ladies, you've got ten minutes!"

She was in her 80's, with silver hair stylishly pulled up on top of her head with a small black bow. She was wearing an oversized, hot pink, starched linen blouse pulled together at the neck with a lavish diamond studded frog. This blouse was over a pair of black tights that were stretched over her size 2 legs and black high heel scuffs. Obviously, a lady of some means and the confidence to go with it!

Under most circumstances, I might have turned around and walked out, but I had taken two samples of drapery fabric earlier that month, had tried both in the room, had decided on one and was ready to make the purchase. This probably wouldn't take more than 10 minutes! The other two girls were not planning to buy anything!

"What can I show you?" the well-coifed owner asked.

"I need some yellow fabric," I said.

"Yellow fabric is right over here," she responded as she dramatically waved her arm in the direction of the yellow fabric.

"How many yards do you need?"

"I need 15 yards of this one." I pointed to the

one that matched the small sample clutched tightly in my hand.

"You'll need 16 yards," she said. "Always repeat the color somewhere in the room. Bob, cut her 16 yards of this yellow fabric."

Bob, a very laid back, older gentleman who had obviously worked here for years and long ago decided not to be intimidated by this lady, slowly picked up the bolt of yellow fabric.

"I don't have 16 yards of this fabric," he said.

"No problem," said the owner. "She'll take this one," pointing to the bolt of yellow next in line.

"You'll love this fabric. It makes up beautifully. Cut her off 16 yards of this one."

I stood there trying to figure out what was going on. They were cutting off 16 yards of the fabric I had decided not to get!

"What else can I show you?" she asked.

"Do you have a black belt strip?" I asked.

"Sure we do. Connie, bring out the belt strips." Connie went to get the belt strips. Before Connie returned, Leigh asked, "Nancy, how do you think this plaid fabric would look on my little bench?" I looked over toward her and said, "I think that would look good."

"How much do you need?" asked the owner.

"Well, the bench is small, probably 1 yard will be plenty," said Leigh.

"Cut her off two yards, Bob. You need to repeat the color somewhere in the room," she said.

"But this bench is in a hall. There is no place to repeat the color," Leigh said.

"Well, you'll find a place, I am sure," the owner concluded.

Connie arrived at the desk with several belt strips. I was planning to purchase only a black one.

"Do you have a belt this color?" the owner asked, showing me a buffed gold.

"No, I don't believe I do." I said.

"Well, you have to have this color. It goes with everything. You'll love it. And what about this brown lizard? Do you have this one?"

"No, I don't have that one either," I said, apologizing.

"Connie, she'll take the black, the gold and the lizard."

In the next room, I heard Ginna say,

"Nancy, what do you think about this lamp?" I walked into the next room, but the owner had gotten there first.

"How do you think this lamp will look with my tulip fabric sofa?" Ginna asked. Before I could say anything, the owner jumped in.

"You know it will look good. You just don't have confidence in your own opinion. How will you be paying for this?" she asked.

"Credit card, I guess," Ginna said.

"Bob! Wrap it up."

At the desk, the owner's daughter, Tweed, and her 5-year-old daughter, Pendleton, were working at closing up the shop but were looking on. Since we didn't know the owner's name, we decided to call her Silk, for she certainly was smooth! I looked at my watch, and it was 5:10 pm. In 20 minutes we had purchased:

- 16 yards of a fabric I didn't want (which was an extra yard as well) @ $15.95 per yard
- 3 belt strips (when I intended to buy one) @ $65.00 each for 2 and $75.00 for 1
- 2 yards of plaid (when Leigh just needed 1 yard) @ $12.00 per yard
- 1 metal tulip lamp (Ginna never intended to purchase) @ $185.00

We made a beeline for the car with all of our purchases. Silk and Tweed followed us out to the car, talking to us all the way.

"I know you are successful," Silk said to me.

"Why would you think that?" I asked.

"Well, you know how to make decisions," she said. I almost laughed. She obviously didn't realize who had been making the decisions for the last 20 minutes!

"I need for you to come teach a class to women in decision making!" Silk continued. "I have women who say they have to talk to their husbands about sofas. You know, I have never met a man who cares about a sofa. He just wants something to sit on!"

We were in the car, when Silk motioned for me to roll down the car window.

"You know, you just need to make a decision and don't look back or you will turn to a pillar of salt." With those last words of wisdom, we drove off. There was silence for a moment. Then I said, "Girls, we have just encountered the Queen of Retail."

10

BAKED 'UM ON THE SQUAT

Emma was one of the cooks at The Glen Rock Inn for many years. One of her jobs was to make the biscuits. Tallulah, an excellent cook in her own right, ate one of Emma's biscuits one day. The biscuit was not as good as usual.

"Emma, what happen to your biscuits?" Tallulah asked.

"They 'rized' and they squat, and I baked 'um on the squat."

11

TWO FINGERS

One summer while Tallulah and C.T. were running the Inn, a new shower needed to be installed in the downstairs bathroom. Two of our friends, Hal and Lynn, said they would run up one afternoon and put the shower in for them. They arrived in the late afternoon on a scorcher of a day. They crawled under the house to begin their project.

They had been under the house for about 45 minutes and were dying of thirst when Tallulah came out on the front porch and called down to the guys.

"Would you like to have a drink?" she asked, in her Southern drawl.

"Yes," they agreed.

"Would you like some bourbon?" she asked.

"Yes," they agreed.

"One finger or two?" she asked.

"Two," they voted.

When she returned with their drinks, they took them and turned the glasses up! To their surprise, Tallulah had not measured with the two fingers quite as they had imagined! They accused her of measuring the depth of the bourbon with her first and fourth fingers rather than first and second!

To their amazement, the shower still works!

12

THE $15,000 FINGER

When the Outback Steakhouse opened locally, everyone fell in love with the bloomin' onions. I was thrilled to discover on a visit to my restaurant supply house that I could purchase a bloomin' onion cutter. I made the $600 purchase and took it to The Glen Rock Inn for a big fourth of July celebration we were planning.

Mike, a friend of the Welch family for many years, was in the kitchen and had helped prepare the onions for the crowd. Everyone had enjoyed the onions and Mike had just finished washing the cutter. As he returned the cutter to the top of the oven, John stepped into the kitchen to brag on how great the onions had been.

"How did you do them, Mike?" John asked.

"Well, you just lift up this handle, you put the onion here, and then…" Before Mike could complete the demonstration, the handle on the cutter slipped out of his wet hand and the surgical steel blades cut right through Mike's fingers. The blades nearly cut off one finger completely and put a deep gash in a second finger.

The good news is that even on the fourth of July, there was a hand surgeon, one of the best in the country, on call at the hospital in Asheville. He was not only able to save the finger, but the finger works as good as new. Of course, the cost for the operation was about $15,000, and we said we were glad Mike had good insurance!

The bloomin' onion cutter still sits in the same place, on top of the oven, but every time anyone asks what it is, we quickly tell the story about Mike's finger. For some reason, they lose interest in seeing a demonstration!

13

RING HER ROOM

For people who have never been to The Glen Rock Inn, you must know how the rooms are equipped. They have no locks on the doors and no TV's or phones in the rooms. Just like the good ole days.

One evening, a guest's husband called and asked,

"Could you please ring Mrs. Coker?"

"Sure, I'll be glad to," I said.

I reached for the dinner bell, rang it several times, then ran upstairs and got his wife!

14

MARIAH

During the summers at the Inn, Tallulah and several of her friends would play bridge a couple of nights a week. Sometimes they would play at the Inn and sometimes they would play at various places in Black Mountain. One night, Sister Segal was going to drive four ladies to the library in Black Mountain to play. She had silver hair and wore it pulled up on top of her head with a small, black velvet bow on the very top. Her late husband had owned the Black Mountain Icehouse. After his death, the icehouse was sold and she lovingly wore the gold skeleton key to the icehouse door on a black velvet ribbon around her neck. Sister Segal was about 4'6" tall and drove a black Hudson. She was so short that she had to look at the road by peering between the steering wheel and the metal ring that was the horn.

Sister Segal picked up Tallulah first and she got in the front seat. Maurice Harrison, whose husband owned the funeral home in Black Mountain, was the next to be picked up. She got in the car and sat directly behind the driver, Sister Segal. Then they pulled up to Mariah's house. Mariah was also less than five feet tall and no matter the weather, always wore a fox fur jacket and a flat hat popped right on the top of her head. This evening was no exception even with the July heat.

Mariah opened the door behind the driver, and Maurice told her to go around. Sister Segal, slightly deaf and not hearing those words, thought Mariah had gotten in. She put the car in reverse and backed up. Maurice started shouting, "You've run over Mariah! You've run over Mariah!"

Sister put the car in forward gear and drove over her again.

They all got out of the car and quickly went to see about their friend. Fortunately, Sister had only run over Mariah's leg. Even though she had run over her leg twice, at least Mariah wasn't dead, but she was very mad! Her words were,

"What in the hell are you trying to do? Kill me"!

15

I DON'T KNOW

Several couples were going to Asheville for dinner one evening, and all we knew about the restaurant was that it was on Highway 23 near the Civic Center. As we came up the hill by the Civic Center, there was a Highway 23 sign with an arrow pointing in both directions. We all said, "Great! Which way do we go, right or left?" Then we looked next to the road sign. There, in the yard of a Catholic church, was a statue of a saint with both hands, palms turned up, shoulders shrugged, as if to say, "Don't ask me. I don't know either!"

16

A CRITICAL SPLIT

One weekend in the fall, we had a group of friends at the Inn for a house party. These parties had become a tradition, and the routine was that the men played golf or watched football on TV and the ladies shopped. This weekend was no exception. We loaded the "girls" up in several cars to go toward Asheville. The ladies in my car wanted to begin their retail experience by visiting some antique shops downtown. I parked on the street, and the three ladies in the back seat slid out one by one. Susan, who had a most attractive figure, was the last one out. As she stepped onto the sidewalk, she said she felt a cool breeze on her "seat"! We all saw why! She felt the back of her shorts and realized she was feeling her underwear! She began saying, "Oh, my! Oh, my"!

Not wanting anyone passing by to witness the horizontal split in her shorts, she backed up to the antique store window. We huddled around the front of her until she could tie a sweatshirt that I kept in the trunk of my car around her waist. We thought all was well! But when we had to step <u>down</u> into the store, we saw a row of husbands standing in front of the window where Susan had been standing with her back to them! They were all smiling as we entered, and we gasped as we realized the show that Susan had provided!

17

BLOOMERS

There were several Southern ladies that for many years, spent their summers at The Glen Rock Inn. Part of the ritual at the Inn was that each morning about 10:00 am, Tallulah would take her lady guests and her hostess, Miss Lena Jones, into Black Mountain to the drug store for a Coke! This was a real treat and one that they did not miss. In the afternoon, after a short nap, the same carload would drive into Asheville to shop at Bon Marché and Ivey's, as well as some specialty shops that featured either hats or shoes. They would park the car on the main street of

Asheville, and they would walk up and down the streets, since all of the stores were close together.

This was in the era of girdles and bloomers or loose panties. Well-dressed women wore a girdle to hold everything in and then loose panties were pulled over the girdle, since the girdles were just tight tubes!

On one of these shopping trips, the ladies were walking from one store to another when Mrs. Kelly's bloomers slid down to the sidewalk! Being a true Southern lady, she looked down, quickly assessed the situation, stepped over them and kept on walking, never missing a beat and never looking back!

18

PICNIC TABLE OR FINE PIANO

The sixty-foot long front porch at The Glen Rock Inn has always been a favorite place to rest. For years, the porch floor had been painted Charleston green or battleship gray. We had continued the painting tradition until the time had finally come when the floor needed to be stripped back to the wood to begin again.

The men that were doing the refinishing called to say that the floor was so beautiful, they didn't want to put paint on again. They said the porch floor was heart of pine and the natural color of the wood was beautiful. I listened to them over the phone but didn't really grasp the magnitude of what they were saying. I explained that the floor took a real beating from all of the guests, plus during the winter, the floor spent many days under snow and rain and needed protection! The painter gave in, and we compromised with wood stain rather than paint. I went to the paint store and selected a <u>light</u> stain called, "Rosewood." I called him back and told him he could pick up enough "Rosewood" for the job at the store.

Several days later, I received a distressed call from the painter. He said they had gone to the paint store and had picked up two gallons of stain. One painter with a bucket of stain had started at one end of the porch, and another painter with another bucket of stain had started at the other end of the porch. When they met in the middle, they discovered they had been given one bucket of Rosewood and one bucket of Redwood!

"One end of your porch looks like a beautiful piano and the other end looks like a K-Mart picnic table!" he said.

We stripped the floors back to the heart of pine and have never used another drop of stain. The painter won!

19

THE BIG THROW AWAY

After the Welches turned the Inn over to Charlie and me, we decided to do some much needed cleaning. We invited some of our friends up for a clean out and clean up weekend! Carol and Lynn took one area of the house, Nancy and Hal worked under the house, others worked in the maintenance closets, in the linen closets, in the kitchen, and in the pantry. Any item that someone thought should be thrown away was tossed without questions asked! The items tossed ranged from an old red leather sofa to bolts and bolts of fabric that would never be used.

Soon after our weekend tossing party was over, we opened the Inn for the season. The Welches drove the cooks up from South Carolina. As they pulled into the yard, Tallulah saw the dumpster, overflowing with "their" stuff. She turned to one of the cooks and said,

"They've thrown it ALL away!"

20

MILAN, MILAN, THE HANDYMAN

I was having the floors refinished in four of the bedrooms in the Inn during the off-season. The young man that was going to do the work was "MILAN, MILAN, THE HANDYMAN." Actually, I had found Milan, a young Russian, through a good friend, Bill.

I had shared bear stories with Bill at various times, so he felt obligated to warn Milan that he might see a bear while in Montreat. Bill told him to be cautious early in the morning when he would go out for breakfast and early in the evening when he would go out for dinner. In spite of the warning, Milan was very excited at the possibility of a bear encounter.

One evening, Milan called Bill.

"Mr. Bill, Mr. Bill! There is a baby bear outside."

"Where is he?" asked Bill.

"He is running around my truck!" said Milan.

"Milan, you must be careful. Even baby bears will bite. Do you understand?"

"Yes, I know. You told me they could be dangerous," said Milan. "Mr. Bill, the bear is so cute. What kind of bear is he? He is black and has a white stripe down his back!"

21

"UH-O-LEG"

Emma was one of the Welches' cooks. She worked for them in Bishopville in their home in the winter and in Montreat in the summer. I was expecting Nelson and with another son, Turner, less than two years old, I knew I would need someone to help me when I came home with the new baby. My mother had passed away just after Turner was born, so Tallulah was next in line! She thought Emma would be more help than she would be, so Tallulah was going to bring her up to stay with me for a couple of weeks when the baby came.

About two or three weeks before Nelson was born, Emma was working at the Welches' home. Tallulah paid her, and she started walking home by way of the liquor store. Apparently, she began sipping on her purchases, so by the time she was several blocks from her home, she was well on her way to being under the influence! Marie, another of the Welches' cooks, was driving home about that time and saw Emma weaving down the sidewalk. Marie stopped, picked her up and gave her a ride the rest of the way.

Marie pulled into Emma's yard. Emma opened the door and got out of the car. In the darkness, Marie did not see that after Emma closed the car door, she passed out on the ground. Marie put the car in reverse and began backing out of the yard. Suddenly, she heard a couple of neighbors screaming and saw them waving their arms trying to get Marie's attention.

"You've run over Miss Emma! You've run over Miss Emma!" the neighbors were shouting.

Marie put the car in drive to pull back in the yard and ran over her again!

They got Emma to the hospital, and her leg was broken in several places. They operated on her leg before she ever woke up from her own anesthesia! Imagine her surprise to wake up in the hospital with a cast from her hip to her toes!

Of course, I was concerned when I heard the news, wondering what I was going to do for help! However, Emma assured Tallulah that by the time the baby came, she would be able to get around and would plan to come to Greer anyway. I told all of my friends what had happened to Emma.

Nelson was born right on schedule. Emma came to take care of us. Turner called her "uh-o-leg," and my friends began arriving to see the newest addition to the family. When they would come to the door, they would say,

"Emma, what happened to your leg?"

She would say,

"I had a car accident!"

22

STRETCHING THE TURKEY

C.T. Welch was always the one who sliced the meat, no matter what the entree. In the early days, he did the slicing with a knife that was like a razor blade. In the latter years, he had an electric meat slicer. Regardless of the method, C.T. could slice turkey so thin you could read the newspaper through it! C.T. could slice a whole turkey so thin he could serve 50 people!

My father talked about going to Rotary meetings in Ocala, Florida, where the "meat at the luncheon was sliced so thin, it only had one side!" C.T. Welch must have trained those folks!

23

THE CAT IN THE CAR

One summer, a mother cat made her home under the Inn. Shortly after we opened in June, she had several kittens. The cook that summer was fond of cats and took very good care of them. But when the summer was over, the mother cat and all but one of the kittens had already disappeared.

Several weeks later, in early fall, our church in Greer had a retreat at the Inn. One of the members of our church is such an animal lover that she defies that description! During the weekend, Anne noticed this little cat hanging around and of course, fed him. As we were all leaving on Sunday afternoon, she said to me,

"The next time you come up here, let me know and I will give you my cat carrier. If you will bring him home, I'll find him a good home." I agreed, but since I am not a cat lover, I didn't grasp the importance of the information about the cat carrier!

One morning in late October, on my way to work, I heard the weather report from WMIT, a Black Mountain radio station. Extreme cold weather and strong winds were coming in that afternoon. I immediately thought about my geraniums, which I try to save from year to year. When I got off work that day, I would go to the Inn and rescue the geraniums.

I drove into the back of the Inn, dressed in a black suit and high heels. I jumped out of the car, dashed into the house and changed clothes to start getting the geraniums under the house before dark. As I was coming down the steps, I heard this mee...ooow. I looked down and there was the little cat. Remembering the request from

Anne to bring him back to Greer, I said to him,

"If you are still here when I finish, I'm taking you to Greer!"

I began making the transfer of the geraniums from the flowerbed to under the house. I changed back into my suit, locked the house and when I got to the car, there, sitting right by the door was the cat! I said, "Okay, get in. We're going to South Carolina."

The cat sat on the front seat until we got to the end of the driveway...not a long way. And then, the perfect gentleman turned into a caged lion! Suddenly he was in the back window, then on the dash board, then on the back seat, then on the back of my neck, then under my feet, then back on the seat, then in the back window! I began to realize the importance of the cat carrier! However, since I didn't have one, I figured the next best avenue was the open door! I pulled over at the post office and opened the car door. I'm sure someone in the area of the post office has had a wonderful pet!

24

SHAMPOO

Dorothy was a quiet, lovely young woman and one of the cooks at The Glen Rock Inn. For several years, she had worked at the Inn in the summer and for the Welches in the winter.

Until 1985, when we took over the Inn and built the apartment at the rear, the cooks had stayed in an out building in the same location. This out building would have reminded you of the row houses found on the cotton or tobacco farms in the lowlands of South Carolina. The house had four bedrooms and one bathroom. The bedrooms were in a row (thus the name) with each one opening to the front, slender porch. The porch was the gathering place for the cooks. Out there you would find several chairs, an ironing board, and all of the items they used to fix each other's hair!

The house was about 50 years old, and nothing had been done in the way of repairs, let alone renovations. There were cracks in the floor, spaces in the walls, doors that did not fit closely with the frames and other structural minuses!

Dorothy had everything cooking in the kitchen for dinner and said she was going to go wash her hair. She went to her bedroom and reached for her bottle of shampoo and there was a snake wrapped around the bottle! Suddenly, quiet Dorothy became wild Dorothy. We heard her screaming as she came running out of the bedroom, onto the porch and into the kitchen of the Inn. Her very dark, chocolate skin had nearly turned white!

A fearless young man got rid of the snake. Then the ritual of snake scaring began. Each cook had her own home remedy for getting rid of snakes. First, we had to get Epsom salt and spread it in a row completely around the house. The belief was that a snake would not cross over a row of Epsom salt. Of course, this one probably came up through the floor, but we didn't try to inject logic into this theory. Second, we had to have fire. The cooks took coffee and soup cans and put oil in the bottom of them along with small scraps of fabric and string and set them on fire. Not until later did I discover they burned the arm cover from one of our chairs! Third, in each room, across the thresholds, we had to spread lime powder as the final snake prevention. How the cooks slept out there that night, I'm not sure.

The good news is that Charlie and I determined the time had come to tear down this "row house" and build an up-to-date building where the cooks could live. As soon as the summer was over, the bulldozer came, and a new four-bedroom apartment was built. The bad news is that since then, the cooks from Bishopville have never returned. The new apartment was just not home.

25

THE BISCUITS

Our next door neighbors at the Inn were having guests for the weekend. Suzanne had prepared some biscuits and in her haste to get to the mountains before her guests arrived, had forgotten them. Sam, known to Montreaters as Greasy, and known to me as my summer paperboy, had been given the assignment to go by the house on his way out of town and get the biscuits.

Sam drove up to the house, and the first question from Suzanne was, "Did you bring the biscuits?" Not wanting to spend the weekend in the doghouse, he stepped right over to the Inn.

"Nancy, do you by chance, have any left over biscuits?" After telling me the story of the biscuits in the freezer back in Charlotte, I knew I had to produce. As luck would have it, we had a full pan of our "Signature" item left over and right out of the oven.

Sam walked out on the porch of the Inn, hollered over to Suzanne and the guests who were standing on their deck!

"You want biscuits? You've got biscuits!"

He carefully carried next door a large tray laden with 96 hot biscuits! Their four guests got plenty of biscuits and a big laugh out of this, but more importantly, Sam stayed out of the doghouse!

26

DO IT YOURSELF SURGERY

Every fourth of July, the "boys" of summer, "OLE Montreaters," have an OLE timers softball game on their "field of dreams," WELCH FIELD. This is the time when, no matter how little exercise these over-50 guys have had for 51 weeks, they are always ready to play ball during the 52nd week.

During the year, they are doctors, lawyers and various kinds of chiefs, but this one day, these boys of summer are remembered by their Montreat nicknames, given to them some 40 years ago. There are names such as: Bird Man,

Geach, H., Greasy, Slimy, Stinky, Gordo, Winkie, Sweets, WaWa, Cannon Ball, John L., Thumper, Red and Jimbo, just to mention a few. With names like these, disaster is inevitable.

Through the years, just about every kind of injury you can imagine has happened during the softball game. There have been pulled hamstrings, turned ankles and bruises in unnamed places. There have been cases of severe sunburn, several dislocated wrists, shoulders and knees, a broken foot and two broken ribs. One year, a guy who couldn't swim chased a fly ball into center field and fell face down in the creek, almost drowning in two inches of water! However, by far, the most challenging injury was the summer that the batter threw his bat behind him and hit Dr. Jimbo in the head. Jimbo was such a trooper that he went across the street from Welch Field to H.'s house and asked for a hand mirror so that he could stitch up his own head! In fact, H. ended up holding the mirror at the right angle so that Jimbo could get the stitches just right! As if that wasn't bad enough, later that evening, Jimbo was "starring" in MONTREAT MADNESS, a skit with old Montreaters as the stars. In Jimbo's role, he had to put a large pot on his head while someone else used the pot for a drum! Everyone in the audience who knew what had happened a few hours earlier cringed each time the pot was hit!

27

CHUBBY

Charlie contracted with a local painter to do some work at the house. The painter was also a minister at a small church. He and his wife were about to celebrate their 25th wedding anniversary, and their congregation was having a reception for them. Charlie and I were invited to the reception, and we arrived a few minutes before the appointed time.

When we entered the social hall, there were a couple of ladies fixing the punch and putting the finishing touches on the food trays. The preacher saw Charlie and motioned for him to come to the other end of the hall where he had a project he wanted to show him. I was standing by the wall trying not to get in the way.

One of the punch ladies, who had a bee hive hair do, saw me standing alone and came over to make me feel welcome.

"I know who you are," she said. "You're Nancy Welch." I agreed that I was.

"I used to watch you on TV. I have had every hair-do that you have had. I used to love to see what you were wearing and what you were cooking. You were just great!" My head began to swell.

Her son, who was probably about eight years old, walked up.

"Do you know who this lady is?" she asked.

He not only didn't <u>know</u> who I was, he didn't <u>care</u> who I was. His mother wouldn't let up.

"You do know who this lady is. You've seen her on TV," the lady insisted. I spoke up and said that I had not been on TV for several years and there was no way this young fellow could know who I was. She returned,

"Oh, we see your commercials on TV. Don't you remember seeing her on the commercial for vinyl siding?" she addressed her son. He took one more long look at me and then said, "You're the lady on TV my mother said has gotten real chubby."

28

THE MOTORCYCLE RIDE

During one of our house party weekends, Ben and Nancee brought two dirt bikes. On Saturday afternoon, several of us decided to take a turn on the bikes. Steve jumped on one bike and asked me to get on behind him. There was already another couple on the other bike, and they had taken off up the street in front of the Inn. We passed them because they didn't know where to go and I didn't want them to get lost on the side of the mountain. When we realized they were not behind us, I suggested we stop and wait for them. My "driver" said we would just turn around, go back and find them. I agreed. So we tried to do a "U" turn in the middle of the road. As we were making the turn, Steve hit the throttle instead of the brake. We both flew into the ditch, the bike turned over on its side, the footrests ripped our pants, the heel broke off of my shoe and generally, we were scratched and banged up. We looked like we had been in a wreck, which we had been!

We got up out of the ditch and tried to determine if any bones were broken. As we brushed ourselves off and tried to get our dignity back, I asked him if he had ever had a wreck on a motorcycle.

"A wreck on a motorcycle? Are you kidding? This is the first time I've ever BEEN on a motorcycle."

29

THE OLDER WOMAN

I was waiting for my daughter-in-law in the parking lot at the entrance to Belk. This summer day, the temperature was in the high 90's and the humidity was just as severe. While sitting there in my car, I noticed an older woman walking up and down the rows of cars. She was obviously hot as a match, wiping her brow with a cloth and looking perplexed. I realized that she had probably forgotten where she had parked her car. Since it was hot and I was in my cool Lincoln Town Car, I wasn't thinking about getting <u>out</u> to help her find her car! I did decide to <u>drive</u> up next to her and see if I could help, without getting out of my car!

"Have you lost your car?" I asked, after I rolled down my window.

"Yes," she said.

"Would you like to get in my car so I can drive you around the parking lot and we will locate your car?"

"No, I'll find it. I know it is here somewhere," she said assuredly.

"Well, there are three entrances to Belk, and they all look just alike," I said. "I'll go around the lot and see if I can find your car. What kind is it?"

"It's a red pick-up truck," the lady said. I thought a red pick-up truck couldn't be too hard to spot. I drove around the parking lot that she was walking, but didn't see a red pick-up truck. I returned to the older lady, whom I could see was getting hotter by the minute.

"Your truck isn't in this parking lot. I'll ride over to the next Belk lot and see if the truck is there," I offered. She said that would be fine. The adjoining lot was on a slight hill, and at the top of the hill, there was a red pick-up truck. I drove over to it. Standing outside the truck, looking down on the parking lot, were two young men in their 20's! I pulled up in my black Lincoln and my bleached blonde hair, rolled my window down and asked, "Are you looking for an older woman?" Without batting an eye, they said, "NO." Realizing what I had just said, I pulled away quickly, hoping neither young man recognized me!

I returned to the woman. She was still walking up and down the parking lot. I told her that her truck wasn't in the lot to the right. She said,

"My husband is in the truck!"

Well, that would have been helpful information five minutes ago! I was not going to be outdone by this OLDER WOMAN.

I drove to the lot on the left side of Belk. There was a red pick-up truck with an old man sitting in it. I got out of my car and went over to him.

"Are you looking for your wife?"

"NO," he said.

"Well, there is a lady in the next lot looking for her husband and she said he is in a red pick-up truck." The man just looked at me but didn't say a word. I walked back and got in my car. When I returned to the first parking lot, the woman had given up the walk and was sitting on a rock wall near the entrance to Belk. I pulled up beside her and rolled down my window.

"Does your husband smoke?" I asked.

"YES HE DOES," she said emphatically.

"Is he wearing a denim jacket?" I asked.

"YES HE IS," she answered.

"Are you from Toccoa, Georgia?"

"YES WE ARE," she said.

"Well, there is a red pick-up truck and a man in the truck that fits that description in the next parking lot," as I pointed over to the left, "but he is NOT looking for his wife!"

30

THE WATERMELONS

During the early years, when the C.T. Welches were running the Inn, Tallulah had a hostess, Miss Lena Jones. Miss Jones was a very tall, stately, unmarried woman. She was a school-teacher by profession so working at the Inn in the summer was the perfect job. Miss Jones was always impeccably dressed with shoes that matched her silk dresses and jewelry that appeared to be custom designed for each outfit.

One of the weekly "chores" for Miss Jones and Tallulah was to drive into Black Mountain to purchase fresh flowers for Miss Jones to arrange. On this particular day, they stopped at their favorite roadside stand to purchase the flowers, and there was an additional item for sale. Over to the side, a man had a table full of watermelons. Miss Jones and Tallulah walked over to his table to look at the melons.

The man stepped right up to them. He wasn't a bad looking man but he did have that weathered look.

"These are beautiful watermelons," said Miss Jones. "I've always said if I could find a man that could raise a watermelon like this, I would marry him," she confessed.

When he heard Miss Jones' confession, he had one of his own! As he smiled, before making his confession, his teeth revealed that several past dental appointments had obviously been missed and his favorite pastime was chewing tobacco. The juice was running out of the corners of his mouth and between the empty spaces where teeth should have been!

"Lady," the man said. "You ain't got to look no further. I rize um."

31

THE YARD SALE

After Charlie and I had run the Inn for a couple of seasons, we realized that storage was at a premium and that the best thing we could do would be to get rid of everything that was not absolutely necessary. The main area of concern was the kitchen where we had old pots and pans that were not used, as well as many dishes that were just taking up space. Many years before, C.T. had gone to the Asheville YMCA when they were closing down and had made quite a haul. From the Y, he had purchased two wooden checkerboard tables, several couches and hundreds of dishes with YMCA printed on them in hunter green letters. The plates were heavy, and we used them for every meal. But the largest crowd we could ever serve was 100 people, so there was no need to have over 200 plates, cups, saucers and cereal bowls. We decided to have a yard sale.

On Saturday morning, we were ready with all of the dishes lined up in the parking lot behind the Inn. We had pots and pans, couches, a lounge chair, bed linens of all kinds and many other items! The first customer drove in with a station wagon. You could tell this wasn't her first rodeo. She knew what she was looking for, and we were ready to let her have it.

"How much do you want for the dishes?" she asked.

"How many do you want? A place setting or just individual dishes?" I asked.

"Well, what would you take for all of them?"

"ALL of them?" I answered with surprise.

"Yes, what kind of price would you charge me if I take all the dishes you have?" I looked at

Charlie, and he looked at me. We were both thinking that we were probably going to have to put them in the dumpster to get rid of ALL of them and here was someone wanting to BUY all of them. Amazing!

"Make us an offer," said Charlie.

"$25.00," she returned.

"We'll take it," said Charlie, not wanting her to change her mind. She turned her car around and backed up to the dishes. Charlie and I filled up the back section, put more on the floor of the back seat and finished by filling up the front seat and floor. We took the money and were pleased as punch! What an idiot she was to buy YMCA dishes, and so many. What in the world would she ever do with all of them? That was not our problem, and we didn't care what she did with them!

Several weeks later, I went to Black Mountain to look through several antique shops. When I got to the back of one of the shops, there was a huge display of YMCA dishes, all arranged in place settings, and each place setting was $25.00!

To add injury to insult, there were several women standing there, counting them out, so as to be sure there were enough dishes for each woman to have several place settings!

I've never had another yard sale.

32

COCONUT PIE

On one of my first trips to The Glen Rock Inn, Mamie, the chief cook, was in the kitchen doing what she did best. She was busy making coconut pies for Sunday lunch. I told her that I wanted to learn how to make them because that was Charlie's favorite kind of pie.

"There's nothing to it. Just watch me," Mamie assured me.

"Take a little shortening," she said, as she scooped her hand down into the huge can of shortening and came up with a small handful.

"Then add some sugar." She made the same

scooping motion with her hand and brought up a larger handful of sugar out of the big bag.

"You will need to add one egg." She broke the egg and put the contents into the bowl.

"Then add a half of an eggshell of milk." I looked at her eggshell. A perfect split. Both halves were exactly the same. I was trying to remember if I had <u>ever</u> broken an egg in such a way that I had enough of a shell big enough to use to measure milk. Hum. No, I don't believe I have. I then told Mamie her recipe was safe. I would just have to let her continue to make coconut pies for Charlie!

33

THE GIRDLE

One hot Sunday, Tallulah went upstairs to dress for lunch. She always started with her girdle which was made out of a heavy rubber, probably ½" thick. There was no top or bottom but rather just a rubber tube. To make struggling into this garment easier, there were many small holes cut in the rubber.

Tallulah had been very busy in the kitchen that morning. Sunday lunch at 12:30 pm was the most important meal of the week. Dinner guests from nearby Black Mountain, as well as outsiders on vacation but not staying at the Inn, would come for lunch after church. The Inn was not air conditioned then so Tallulah was perspiring!

She sat down on the edge of the bed, put the girdle on the floor, stepped both feet in, stood up and began to pull the rubber tube over her hot, perspiring body. Since underwear and hose were to be worn <u>over</u> this tube, Tallulah was pulling the girdle up over her perspiring skin! The process went well as she worked the tube over her calves. When she got to her thighs and hips and slightly protruding stomach, the going was slower. The harder she pulled, the hotter she got. She was running out of time, for in just a few minutes, her dinner guests would be arriving downstairs. The more frustrated she got, the more she perspired. The more she perspired, the less she could move the rubber across her body. She admitted defeat, realizing that getting this on was an impossible task and she had run out of time.

She tried to get the rubber trap off. Quickly, she knew that pulling the tube down was just as impossible as pulling the tube up! She was stuck! Tallulah went to the window that was over the kitchen. She began calling to C.T. for help, but he couldn't hear a word. Walking like a Chinese, taking small baby steps, Tallulah walked to the bedroom door and called down the steps for C.T. Still, he could not hear her. Time was getting shorter, and everyone would soon wonder where she was. By this time, she was just hoping that C.T. would wonder where she was and come upstairs to look for her!

Tallulah continued to struggle with the vice, pulling up getting half of her energy and pulling down getting the rest. This tug-o-war continued until finally C.T. bolted through the door.

"Tallulah, what's the matter? There are people downstairs." As soon as he had spoken, he saw what was the matter and tried to keep from laughing.

"I'm STUCK! This thing won't go up and it won't go down. I've been calling you for 20 minutes, but I knew you couldn't hear me and obviously, I couldn't come downstairs!" she said, out of frustration! Her hair, which she had fixed at the beauty shop in Black Mountain the day before was dripping wet!

"I'll fix you right up. Don't worry," said C.T. He went to the bathroom and got his foot powder! He began pulling the rubber away from her skin and shaking the powder down in the small spaces. Gradually, he made his way around her torso. Meanwhile, downstairs, people were coming in for lunch. Upstairs, Tallulah was a human pillow and C.T. was trying to shake her out of the pillowcase!

Tallulah finally made it into the dining room in plenty of time for <u>dessert!</u>

34

THE PRODUCE MAN

In the early 50's, there was a mountain man that had a produce wagon. He would bring the wagon to the back of The Glen Rock Inn and also next door to Mrs. Robinson's "Camp Gallant." Both Mrs. Robinson and Tallulah looked forward to his visits several times a week as he had beautiful produce!

One summer, the man did not come. Mrs. Robinson and Tallulah did not know how to contact him to find out what had happened.

One day, the following summer, the man's daughter brought the wagon to the back of the Inn.

Tallulah ran out to talk to her and to see the produce.

"We missed your father last summer," Tallulah said.

"Where is he?"

The daughter replied,

"He rize. He spit. He drapt."

35

SWINGING AT NIGHT

C.T. Welch had respiratory problems as he got older, and some nights he would have to give up trying to sleep in his bed. Instead, he would go downstairs and sleep in his lounge chair.

One of those evenings, as he was trying to sleep in the chair, he heard some giggling and whispering coming from the big swing on the front porch. He knew at 3:00 am everyone should be asleep. He opened the front door and inquired about what was going on. To his surprise, a very young couple, in the buff, was in the swing with only a blanket and a pillow between them! As

C.T. shamed them into fleeing, the young man took the pillow and the young girl took the blanket. They disappeared to their separate rooms. I'm sure they hoped that Mr. Welch would not recognize them with their clothes <u>on</u> at breakfast the next morning.

36

THE DRAIN BOARD

One weekend, I had an all-girl house party. Before leaving for dinner in the early evening, we had enjoyed some snacks and beverages in the gazebo while waiting for everyone to dress.

When we returned from Black Mountain, several hours later, a new house party member greeted us! Sitting on the dishwasher drain board was a raccoon. Belle got a mop and tried to encourage him to get down. Alice stood with the door open in front of her so he had a clear shot at freedom. Brenda stood in the doorway to the kitchen so that she could keep him from entering the rest of the house. After much encouragement from Belle with the mop head, Mr. Raccoon eased over toward the door and went outside right past Alice. He headed straight for the gazebo, where he enjoyed snacks and beverages left behind by the girls!

37

THE FOILED
FOOD FIGHT

I have always been amazed at the chaperones that accompany young people attending youth conferences in Montreat. Just ordinary members of a local church that volunteer to take a week of their vacation to be with the kids. Surely these people have a reserved seat in heaven for putting themselves through torture for a week in the name of Christian youth!

I am never, however, amazed if the chaperones are ministers or directors of Christian education because, after all, that is their job! One year, I was not amazed. I was shocked!

After lunch, I was walking around the outside of the Inn, as I often did, picking up trash the kids had thrown off of the front porch. By the side of the steps, tucked into the ivy, was a plastic bag from the Montreat Bookstore. I picked up the bag and the contents were very heavy. I immediately thought that someone had purchased some books and they had fallen off of the porch railing. I opened the bag and was stunned to discover about two dozen squares of orange fruit Jell-O that had been the salad at lunch that day. I took the bag to the kitchen and disposed of it.

During the spaghetti dinner that night, one of the local patrons was eating with us. She caught my eye as I was passing through the dining room and pulled me over to her.

"Nancy, that man over there has been going from table to table putting all of the leftover spaghetti in a plastic bag."

"The white haired man?" I asked.

"Yes, that man right over there," as she

pointed. "We have been sitting here watching him wondering if he would come to our table and get <u>our</u> leftovers. I wanted to ask him what he was going to do with the food."

"Well, I am thankful you told me," I said. I walked over to him and asked for the bag of spaghetti.

"Dr. Bill," I said, "What are you doing with the spaghetti? Are you planning a food fight?"

"Well," he hesitated, "Yes, but we weren't going to do it here at your place."

"It doesn't matter <u>where</u> you were going to do it," I told him rather sternly. "Anything in Montreat affects <u>everyone</u> in Montreat. You know, there are some people who don't want youth conferences here anyway, and this is part of the reason why. And <u>you</u> are a minister! What kind of an example do you think this is for our youth?" After I had given him a piece of my mind, which I really couldn't do without, he apologized and said they wouldn't have the food fight. As he turned to walk out of the dining room, I said, "Oh, by the way. I'm the one that got the Jell-O."

38

BEARS

For several years, Montreat has had a love - hate relationship with the local bears. Everyone is scared of what they might do but is thrilled when they have guests and the bears show up, lending credibility to their stories. Our son, Turner, was one that was glad to see a bear while he and his wife, Heather, hosted a New Year's weekend house party. Turner had told his buddies about the bears, and as they returned from dinner, the doubting Thomases saw for themselves!

Another time, early one morning, I heard the lid of the dumpster at the rear of the Inn crash. That was a sure sign that there was a bear in the yard. I pulled back the shade on the window and there he was, helping himself to a bag of our garbage. He brought his bag over and sat right under my window to enjoy. I peered at him through the window trying to comprehend that there was only a piece of glass between us.

He finished that bag and went back for seconds. This bag he decided to enjoy right at the base of the dumpster. From my window, I could not see him, so I decided to walk outside and get a better look.

I walked around the edge of the house and peeked from the corner. There he was. His black body was huge with arms and legs as big as a person's torso. His snout had a light brown stripe around it. I wondered if that was a male or female marking, but I thought better than to get close enough to find out. As it was, I was only about ten feet away.

Suddenly, he dropped the bag he was working on, and I jumped back. I figured he heard something…like my heart beating. Then he headed for the woods like a jet.

The same bear returns several times a week even now. His pattern is the same. The first bag of garbage is eaten between the Inn and the Sloan's house next door. The second bag is eaten at the dumpster! Creatures of habit…all of us!

Another time, a man was sitting on the gazebo about dusk, reading the paper. He heard a little splashing of water and when he looked up, a bear was coming right up out of the creek and on to the gazebo. I was inside the Inn and heard him screaming. He bolted through the door, shouting, "There's a bear in the gazebo. There's a bear in the gazebo!" By the time I got out the door, the bear was long gone. He was probably scared of the screaming man, also!

Another evening, I had gone to dinner with friends. Earlier that day, I had cleaned up after the bear, so I was surprised to return and see trash around the dumpster. I commented that the bears must have been back. Newton put on his bright lights. Just then Jacqueline saw the bear sitting on top of the dumpster, eating. At that moment, the bear turned around, leaped to a tree behind the dumpster and started up. However, he didn't get too far up the tree when he decided his best bet was on foot. He slid down and took off into the woods. To be so large, they certainly can move fast!

On yet another evening, several of us were returning from grocery shopping. One of the young men that worked at the Inn was with me and the others were following behind us in a second car.

Blake and I began to unload the groceries.

"Wouldn't it be terrible if we saw a bear and Leigh and Brandon, who want to see one so much, were not here?" I said.

"Yes," Blake agreed. "They would never forgive us!" We were only about ten feet from the dumpster as we unloaded the trunk of the car and had already made several trips to the kitchen.

The other car pulled in and Leigh and

Brandon began screaming,

"Run, Run! There's the bear. There's the bear."

I dropped two gallons of milk, ran over Blake and turned my ankle trying to get in the house! Sure enough, the whole time we were unloading the car, a cub bear was down inside the dumpster and the mother bear was standing beside the dumpster, reaching in with her head to eat! Leigh honked the horn and the bears ran into the woods. A little too close for comfort.

39

THE LOOK

I was in a shop near the Inn and was settling up with the owner. She looked at me with a strange glance. As I turned to leave, she stopped me.

"What is your name?" she asked.

"Nancy Welch," I replied.

"I thought so," she said. "I used to watch you on TV and you look just like yourself!"

40

A TIGER

When our son, Nelson, was being recruited by Clemson University to play football, we were anxious to know if he had been accepted. Clemson had offered him a scholarship, but they were waiting on his SAT scores before he could be accepted. Nelson and Turner, our other son, were at the Inn helping us clean up.

We had been waiting for the call from Clemson to say they had gotten the scores and he was in. The phone rang and the lady on the other end said, "You've got a TIGER." I screamed at the top of my lungs, "We've got a TIGER!" Just then the screen door on the front porch opened, and a lady that had been sitting out there enjoying the rocking chairs said, "Where's the Tiger? I knew Montreat had bears, but I certainly didn't know they had Tigers, too."

41

THE AUCTION

In the old days of Montreat, the evening entertainment was the square dance at the skating rink on Friday nights and the auction in Black Mountain. Mr. and Mrs. Robert Brand would come up from Florida each summer and run their auction. They would return to Palm Beach and do the same thing there in the winter. Tallulah or Mrs. W., as Mr. Brand affectionately called her, loved the auction and would take a car full of guests just about every night. She particularly loved the silver items, china, linens, crystal, and jewelry. Come to think of it, Mrs. W. loved everything Mr. Brand sold!

To keep the audience from going to sleep between items they were showing for bids, they would pass out tickets for door prize drawings. Bob was in charge of the door prizes. His <u>real</u> job was working at Harrison's Funeral Home in Black Mountain, and he had the personality to go with the <u>real</u> job.

When the crowd got quiet, Bob would suggest to Mr. Brand that it was time for a door prize. Mr. Brand would always agree since that gave him an opportunity to go in the back and get something to drink and smoke a cigarette!

The door prizes ranged from plastic rain caps that were folded like an accordion to fingernail clippers in plastic envelopes with snaps on the front! Bob would call a number and hold up the item. No one would speak a word.

"You MUST claim your prize," he would say. Mrs. W. would always get tickled at this part of the evening and whisper under her breath about the quality of the door prizes! But the prizes never improved. The auction was good entertainment. If Mrs. W. didn't talk you into buying <u>something</u>, the entertainment was not only good, but was also free!

42

THE SKUNK

We had been notified that we had to install a fire alarm system in the Inn with smoke detectors in each room. The man that came to inspect the installation was a man about 6'6" tall, thin, wearing skin tight blue jeans, cowboy boots and a large, black, ten gallon hat! He completed his inspection inside the house and then went under the house.

Under the Inn was not a place anyone would want to go! The crawl space was truly just that, crawl space. The dirt and rock "floor" would make the strongest and most daring a bit uneasy.

The man finished his inspection and came back inside to give me the papers.

"You've got a great big, dead skunk under the house," he said with a cocky tone in his voice.

"Really? Where is he?" I asked.

"Right in the middle of the house. For a hundred dollars, I'll pull him out for you," as he continued his attitude.

"A hundred dollars? You must be kidding! For a hundred dollars," I said, "I'll go under the house and get him!"

Meanwhile, another man, Ed, was redoing the kitchen pantry. He heard the conversation and when the fire alarm man left, Ed said <u>he</u> would go under the house and get the skunk for nothing!

Ed crawled under the house with a plastic bag in hand. In a few minutes, I heard him calling.

"Nancy, throw down another bag, and can you find me a box?"

"Sure, Ed. I'll find a box and I'll bring it down."

I found a box and took the bag and box to the

edge of the darkness under the house. In just a minute, I heard Ed crawling back toward the light. I began to smell the skunk and went inside.

Ed disposed of the skunk, double bagged and in the box. When he came in the kitchen, he said, "The man was right! That _was_ worth a hundred dollars!"

43

YOU'RE NOT LOST

During the time I was on TV, I set up an appointment one day to meet with a lady that lived in the mountains. I had the directions to her house in front of me, but I was lost! The winding roads and very few road signs made my trek frustrating. Since I was not familiar with the area, I knew I needed to stop for help.

I spotted a little house off the paved road with a white picket fence and no visible dogs! I pulled into the yard to ask directions. When I stepped up on the front porch, I knocked on the door. An elderly woman opened the door just wide enough to see who it was.

"Please excuse me," I said, "but I am lost."

She looked at me again, through the small crack in the door. Then she threw the door wide open and said in her unmistakable mountain accent, "Why, you ain't lost, you NANCY WELCH!"